A SCARY STORY

WRITTEN
and
ILLUSTRATED BY
PETER BAILEY

Hippo

Tina   Tom

That's us!
We're going to look for
the GHOST OF GRIM GRANGE.

We need . . . a torch,
some warm clothes
and scarves,

some cat-food sandwiches,
and some tomato soup in a flask,

and a knapsack.
Off we go!

It's jolly dark out here!

The gates!

GRIM GRANGE!

Push open the creaky door . . .

up the creaky stairs . . .

along the gloomy corridor . . .

the dusty bedroom . . .

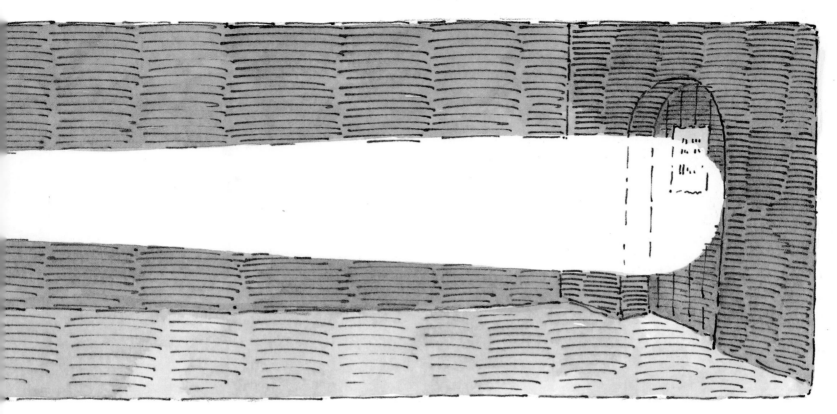

Run! Run! Run!

Down the creaky stairs . . .

and over the hills . . .

to home.
(And the soup and sandwiches.)